This book is a work of fiction. Names, characters, places, and incidents are either the product of the author's imagination or used fictitiously.
Hardback - ISBN: 978-1-923567-48-1

Paperback - ISBN: 978-1-923567-49-8

eBook - ISBN: 978-1-923567-50-4

Cover design by **Holly Symons**
First Edition

For More, Please Visit

HollySymons.com.au

Flameborn Presents

Sarcasm, Sabotage & Other Misfires

(Collector's Edition)

By Holly Symons

Collector's Edition Dedication

To every reader who has walked beside me through fire, chaos, and laughter this book exists because of you. Your belief keeps the flame alive, and your love of story bridges the realms.

To all who dare sip from the Tavern of Tangents may your cups always refill, your tickets never tear, and your laughter echo longer than any warning lamp's glow. Step carefully between the realms, for the pages themselves are alive.

To the fans if reality glitches, blame yourselves. You asked for more mischief, and Loki was listening. Consider this edition both a gift and a gentle warning.

The
Realmbridge
Program

A Dramatic Welcome to Flameborn Presents: Sarcasm, Sabotage & Other Misfires

WELCOME, TRAVELER

You stand at the threshold of a cross-realm cabaret where unspoken feelings burst into ballads, and emotionally unstable squirrels wield swords with flair.

This is not your typical story.
Tonight's program includes heartbreak, haikus, spontaneous glitter combustion, and at least one raccoon legally classified as a fire hazard.

Program Notes & Viewer Warnings

- May contain rogue improv scenes, unsupervised emotional monologues, and passive-aggressive dragons.
- Audience members have reported laughter, tears, and mild existential clarity.
- Please keep hands, tails, and magic artifacts inside the story at all times.
- If Loki rewrites your scene, we cannot offer refunds.

Tavern of Tangents – Drinks Menu

Welcome to the Tavern of Tangents, where the drinks are strong, the stories are stranger, and the menu may or may not rearrange itself mid-order. Please drink responsibly or don't. Loki's running the bar tonight.

Featured Drinks

Glitterbomb Elixir

Sparkling, unpredictable, and slightly sentient. May cause sudden karaoke.

Soul Frost Martini

Distilled from emotionally repressed ice spirits. Served with a ghost of your ex.

Dragon's Breath Toddy

Hot, smoky, and mildly flammable. Drink at your own risk (and not near curtains).

Moonberry Meltdown

Made from nightshade berries and lunar tears. Tastes like your last heartbreak sweet, with a bitter finish.

Nutters' Nerve Tonic

A jittery blend of espresso, panic, and squirrel adrenaline. Guaranteed to keep you up for three days.

Sir Crumbs' Spiked Chai

Warm, cozy, and slightly illegal in three realms. Comes with a glittery top hat stirrer.

Loki's Reality Twist

What flavour? Yes. Served in a cup that occasionally blinks. May cause identity crises.

Main Cast

- Aurelya: The Flameborn - celestial heroine with wings that appear during realm travel; destined protector of the Realms.
- Loki: The Trickster - chaotic best friend, unpredictable and fiercely loyal. Brings humour, heart, and occasional squirrel-related chaos.
- Odin: The All-Father - complex, tormented, and absurdly dramatic. Hangs himself from a tree to find wisdom.
- Fraya: Queen of the 10th Realm - powerful, poised, and deeply healing. Wields both sass and ceremonial glitter.
- Roarnan: The Lion - Aurelya's guardian and emotional compass. Roars in lowercase. Occasionally wears sashes.
- The Dragon: Silent protector and source of power. Merges with Roarnan in times of crisis.

- Gerald: Tragic romantic - emotional support vampire. Drinks bloodtinis and feels deeply.
- Thor: Chaos god with a soft side. Wielder of emotional chickens. Occasionally musical.
- Loki's Squirrel: Unhinged. Weaponizes acorns. May be a chaos deity in disguise.
- Chad: Goblin life coach and clipboard enthusiast. Occasionally the judge, therapist, and party planner.
- Aurexia: Aurelya's mirror-self - composed of rewritten choices, darker magic, and unhealed wounds.
- The Plot Baby: Reality-rewriting toddler with jam-covered fingers and omnipotent power.
- Plottie: The Plot Child - speaks in foreshadowing, eats worldbuilding notes, cries when you skip exposition.

Supporting & Notable Cast

- Clarence: The Lion (true name) - emotionally literate, loves muffins, suspiciously wise.
- The Book Tree: Sentient narrative tree - grows books, screams during edits.
- The Author: Wears redline robes, edits with dramatic flair, mid-life plot crisis.
- The Mirror: Reflects possible versions of the self - and trauma.
- The Plot Court Jury: Includes Sir Broodington III, Rhymelda, Gary, Tina the Tax Auditor, and a sentient sword.
- The Villain Ex: Forgotten subplot. Hot. Wields unsent letters as weapons.

- The Forgotten Gerald: Mirror Gerald - was kissed by Loki to win a bet.
- Princess Rhymelda: Rhymes everything. Terrifying.
- Tina: Time-traveling tax auditor from a deleted dystopia.
- Gary: The guy who almost had an arc.
- Sparkles Roarworthy: Lion in a tiara. Voted Miss Plot 2019.

Table of Contents

Flameborn Presents:

Sarcasm, Sabotage & Other Misfires

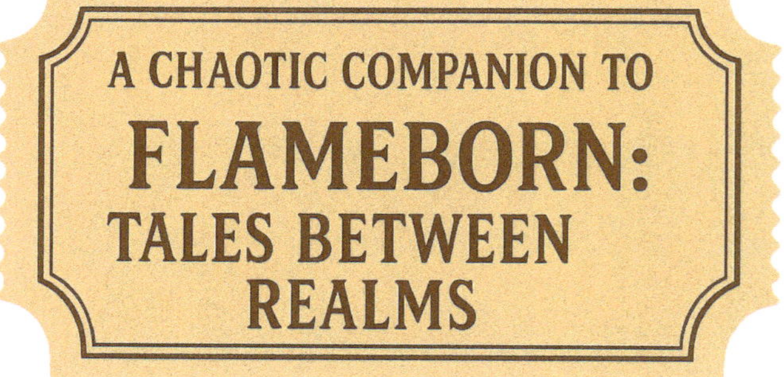

Compiled from inter-realm cabarets, crying circles, and spontaneous sword fights.

SQUIRREL!

THE MUSICAL

Cast Bios

Nutters McFluff (He/Him)

Known throughout the lower realms as the only squirrel to survive a glitter explosion *and* headline an interpretive dance funeral. Nutters began his career scavenging theatre scraps and performing monologues to peanut shells. He was discovered by Loki mid-breakdown (Loki's, not his) and cast instantly. When not performing, Nutters can be found writing emotionally devastating acorn poetry and sword-fighting his imposter syndrome.

Sir Crumbs (He/Him)

A reformed raccoon warlord turned tap-dancing therapist. After leading the infamous "Snack Sack Rebellion," Crumbs found inner peace (and jazz shoes) and now channels his aggression through sequins and song. He refuses to discuss the incident with the meat pie, but critics agree: "Sir Crumbs can pirouette through trauma like no one else." He has three honorary degrees, all from fake universities.

Loki Laufeyson

Cast Bio (Framed Backstage Version)

THIS PLAQUE WAS NAIL-GUNNED

TO THE WALL WITH A GLITTER DAGGER

"I was forced to write this bio under duress and deadline. I reject the concept of labels, formatting, and biographies in general. However, since this book insists on linearity, allow me to summarize:

I am the director, choreographer, creative visionary, chaos incarnate, and the *only* reason this production didn't devolve into interpretive fog and unpaid puppetry.

Previous credits include: Betrayal (ongoing), Shapeshifting (award-winning), and Godhood (revoked twice, reinstated thrice).

If you dislike the show, please complain to someone else.

If you *do* like the show, you're welcome."

~ **Loki Laufeyson**, Artistic Menace and Accidental Director

ACT I: Bar Fights & Self-Discovery

Loki's Guide to Tavern Etiquette for Misfits

A condescending masterclass on how not to get punched (or emotionally attached) in a magical tavern.

Clarence the Lion Goes on a Speed Date with a Sea Witch

He just wanted love. She wanted his soul. It's going... oddly well.

Loki vs. The Minotaur: A Tavern Review Saga

One star. Would not survive again. A dramatic retelling of an extremely avoidable food fight.

Sir Spikeston's TED Talk: 'Self-Care for Spiny Bartenders'

An emotional rollercoaster from a cactus-person with trauma, tea, and exfoliating advice.

Loki's Guide to Tavern Etiquette for Misfits

A barely sanctioned guide by Loki Laufeyson, who insists he's never been kicked out of a tavern 'on purpose.'

Rule #1: Enter Like You Own the Realm

Confidence is key. Even if you tripped on the doormat. Especially if you tripped on the doormat.

Rule #2: Never Sit Near the Fireplace

Unless you're looking to be part of someone's dramatic backstory. Spoiler: it involves betrayal, dragons, or both.

Rule #3: Avoid Eye Contact with Bards

They feed on emotional vulnerability. Blink once and suddenly your heartbreak is a ballad with choreography.

Rule #4: Tip in Gold, Lies, or Favors

Bartenders know things. Pay them creatively. Just don't offer 'exposure', this isn't Instagram.

Rule #5: If the Furniture Starts Talking, Leave

You've either had too much, or the tavern's cursed. Possibly both. Do not engage in political debate with the barstools.

Rule #6: Always Compliment the Cook

Especially if the cook is a troll named Agnes who wields a ladle like Thor's hammer. You don't want to be soup.

Rule #7: Don't Summon Anything Before Happy Hour

There are rules for a reason. Demonic incursions at brunch are frowned upon.

Rule #8: Misfits Stick Together

You're weird. So are they. Buy the raccoon a drink. Let the dragon vent. Nobody belongs here, that's why it works.

Final Thought:

Chaos is inevitable. May as well toast to it.

Clarence the Lion Goes on a Speed Date with a Sea Witch

A tragic romance. A magical misunderstanding. And one emotionally available lion who just wants a plus one for his next realm merge.

Clarence adjusted his tie.

It was his first speed dating event since the Realm of Fire incident, and technically, that one didn't count. He'd been cursed into a wardrobe for most of it.

Across from him sat a woman with sea-foam hair, eyes like shipwrecks, and a smile sharp enough to gut a god.

"Name?" she asked.
"Clarence. I... roar professionally."

She blinked. "You roar?"

"And emotionally regulate."

The sea witch gave a noncommittal nod and stirred her drink with a live eel. "Trauma?"

"Repressed. But I journal now."
The eel burped bubbles.

Clarence tried to smile. "You?"

"Hexed my last boyfriend into a clam. Now I do shadow work."

He nodded. "Healthy."

"You ever fought a kraken with your bare paws?"

"No, but I've comforted one through a

breakup."

For the first time, she smiled.

Somewhere in the Realm of Tangents, a harp played softly. The lights dimmed. The next date was called.

But neither of them moved.

Clarence sipped his drink. It tasted like regret and sea salt.

"So…" he said, glancing at her eel. "What's he like when he's not working?"

"Cuddly," she said.

Clarence smiled. "Good. I don't trust eels who don't cuddle."

Loki vs. The Minotaur: A Tavern Review Saga

One star. Would not survive again. A dramatic retelling of an extremely avoidable food fight, as written by Loki himself.

Name of Establishment: The Horn & Shank Tavern
Date of Visit: Chaotic
Ambience: Dimly lit, emotionally tense, smelled like singed beef.

Let me preface this by saying I was *invited*. I did not crash this tavern. I merely stumbled into it with grace, sarcasm, and a slight flair for mischief. The Minotaur, however, was already six pints into a tantrum and trying to arm-wrestle the moon.
I ordered the house special. It blinked at me. I blinked back. Mutual respect was established.

Then came the fight.

To be clear, I did *not* throw the first drink. I did, however, weaponize a breadstick with the velocity of a minor deity.

The Minotaur countered with a chair.

Audience reaction: mixed. One dwarf cried. A bard started writing a song mid-chaos. A goblin began selling snacks.

The bartender asked us to leave. I left a review instead.

☆☆☆☆

Would not recommend unless you enjoy spontaneous furniture-based violence and beef stew with emotional baggage.

On the plus side: chairs were sturdy.

- Loki Laufeyson, Patron of Drama & Yelp Warlock

Sir Spikeston's TED Talk: Self-Care for Spiny Bartenders

Because even cactus-folk need boundaries, bubble baths, and bartending gloves.

"Welcome, everyone," said Sir Spikeston, clearing his throat and adjusting his cactus bow tie.

"Today, I want to speak from the heart. And the elbow. And occasionally the knee, because that's where the worst bar bruises land."

A polite cheer from the audience.

"I have worked 97 nights straight at the Tavern of Tangents. I've poured drinks for vampires, caught goblins making out in the storeroom, and defused a poetry duel between a banshee and a werewolf. And what did I learn?"

He paused dramatically.

"Moisturize. Daily. Especially your spikes."

A cheer. A single tear from someone in the back row.

"Next, boundaries. Just because you can mix a Moonfire Martini with one hand while catching a cursed dagger mid-air with the other, doesn't mean you should."

"Thirdly: never, and I mean *never*, date someone who orders a Glitter Fizz and doesn't tip. You deserve sparkle *and* respect."

"And finally," he said, holding up a cactus-shaped mug, "hydrate. Because you can't pour from an empty jug. And because tequila is not a substitute for therapy."

The crowd rose to their feet.

Sir Spikeston bowed, his spikes catching the light.

"Thank you. I'll be behind the bar if anyone needs a hug, a drink, or a laminated boundary statement."

ACT II: Songs of the Wounded & Unwell

For those who sing with cracked voices, broken hearts, and receipts from questionable choices.

Blood & Ballads: A Vampire's Guide to Heartbreak and Harmony

Because even the undead deserve a good cry and a killer chorus.

Gerald's Live Podcast Recording & Public Crying Circle

Welcome to episode 347: 'Feelings Are Weird (But Valid)'.

Blood & Ballads: A Vampire's Guide to Heartbreak and Harmony

Because even the undead deserve a good cry and a killer chorus.

Scene: A velvet-curtained lounge inside the Tavern of Tangents. Low lighting. A vampire in crushed burgundy velvet steps onto a tiny candlelit stage. He's holding a microphone, a rose, and centuries of emotional baggage.

Vladislav the Bittersweet: "Welcome to Blood & Ballads. Tonight's set includes heartbreak, betrayal, and a brief stint in Transylvanian jazz."

He gestures dramatically to the band of brooding werewolves in tuxedos.

"First song: 'You Said Forever (But Then You Staked Me)'."

The crowd snaps instead of claps. It's that kind of night.

"Next up: 'Garlic in My Soul (Ballad of the Broken-hearted Buffet)'."
Someone sobs softly into a chalice.

"And to close… the crowd favorite: 'Let Me In (Your Heart and Also Your Castle)'."

As the final notes echo, Vlad bows with theatrical despair and vanishes in a puff of glitter.

A note is left behind on the mic stand:

'Tip your bartenders. Tell your exes nothing. And always harmonize your howls.'

Gerald's Live Podcast Recording & Public Crying Circle

Welcome to episode 347: 'Feelings Are Weird (But Valid)'

Gerald, a half-elf with a podcast voice so soothing it's suspicious, adjusts his headphones and clears his throat.

"Hello, beautiful beings. Today's topic is: It's Okay to Cry at the Tavern , Even if You Just Dropped Your Pie."

Behind him, a semicircle of chairs is filled with fae, dwarves, one anxious griffin, and a goblin wearing a 'Feelings Are Real' badge.

Gerald continues: "We'll begin with a mindfulness exercise called 'Let the Screaming Out, But Like...Softly.'"

The griffin weeps. The goblin hands it a sparkly tissue.

"Now we're going to play a little game: 'Guess That Repressed Emotion.'"

From the back of the room, someone yells, 'ABANDONMENT ISSUES!'

Gerald smiles. "Good start. Now say it as a haiku."

A drumbeat cues the outro music. The tavern lights dim to a gentle purple.

"Thanks for joining. Remember, your vulnerability isn't a weakness, it's a vibe."

He signs off with a nod to the crowd.

"…And next week, we'll be joined by Chad the Goblin Life Coach for a live therapy roast."

ACT III: Sarcasm & Sabotage The Cabaret Series

Hosted by Loki. Produced by Sheer Audacity.

Scene: The lights rise on a crooked velvet stage held together by glitter and spite.

A raccoon in a feather boa is juggling daggers. A goblin is testing the mic with interpretive screaming.

Then Loki appears, dramatically late, wearing a crown made of broken tiaras and poor decisions.

Loki: "Tonight's theme is 'regret, revenge, and musical numbers you probably shouldn't perform sober.'"

He gestures wildly.

"Each act is a live emotional exorcism , so hold your applause until after the meltdown."

Performances include:

- A banshee opera about her toxic ex.
- Tap-dancing skeletons in glitter bow ties.
- A power ballad duet between a disgraced knight and the sword that dumped him.

Loki bows. The glitter explodes. The lights short-circuit.

"And now… please enjoy our signature cocktail: The Spite Spritz. Garnished with your dignity."

A Chaotic Cabaret

Hosted by Loki. Produced by Sheer Audacity.

The stage is unstable. The audience is unstable. Loki is... definitely unstable.

He struts out in a rhinestone cloak and announces, "Tonight's cabaret will include emotional sabotage, interpretive swordplay, and one raccoon burlesque that nobody approved but we're doing anyway."

The spotlight flickers.
The curtain tries to leave.
The show begins.

First Act: A song titled 'Oops, I Set Fire to Your Feelings' - performed by a phoenix in therapy.
Second Act: A comedy sketch where Loki plays

every character in a breakup, including the plant.

Third Act: A literal roast - someone summoned an elemental.

Loki twirls, glitter explodes.
"This is either art or a lawsuit waiting to happen," he says. "Either way, no refunds."

The show ends with a group scream and a glitter avalanche.

Nobody knows what it meant.
Everybody claps anyway.

Breakup Haikus & Accidental Summoning's

Workshop Description:

What began as a casual open-mic night for poetry quickly spiralled into a magical disaster after someone rhymed 'regret' with 'demonic debt.'

The audience was advised not to read anything aloud written in blood, glitter ink, or passive-aggressive cursive.

Sample Haikus:

You ghosted again.
Now there's a squid in my sink.
Thanks for the trauma.

Left your hoodie here.

It grew teeth and tried to bite.
Still smells like bad dates.

Swore you'd never change.
But now you're a warlock, Jeff.
That counts as a change.

Summoning Safety Tips:

- Never rhyme 'forever' with 'never' near candles.
- Glitter is a known portal activator.
- If the ex-responds via mirror… run.

Hosted by Loki. Blame him for everything.

Songs You Wrote About Them (Before They Turned Evil)

Welcome to the saddest, and sassiest, songwriting circle in all the realms.

Tonight's theme: love songs that aged like milk.

Loki introduced the evening with a piano ballad titled:
"I Thought You Were My Twin Flame (Turns Out You Were Just Arson)."

Other notable entries included:
• "You're the Spell I Should've Checked Twice" - performed by a banshee quartet.
• "We Were Magic Until You Hexed My Cat" - featuring harp, scream flute, and guilt.

• "My Heart, Your Sword Collection" – painfully literal.

Aurelya sang briefly, then vanished under a stage trapdoor Loki definitely installed for emotional exit flair.

Audience reviews were mixed:

• The goblins cried.

• The ghosts harmonized.

• The enchanted mic started smoking halfway through.

Finale: All performers joined for a tear-streaked group song called
"Was It Love or a Temporary Magical Binding Agreement?"
(Spoiler: It was both.)

Letters You Wrote But Never Sent (And Definitely Shouldn't Read Out Loud... But Will Anyway)

Every realm has one rule:
Do not read emotionally unstable letters out loud.
Especially during a thunderstorm. Especially near mirrors.

So naturally, Loki made it a main event.

Letter Highlights:

- 'Dear You, I hope your tea always goes cold and your socks never match.'
- 'I regret nothing. Except maybe introducing you to my therapist and my chaos wolf.'
- 'You made me believe in forever. Then ghosted. Now I believe in revenge playlists.'

Halfway through, someone summoned their ex by accident.
They had to duel in limericks.

The raccoon ran tech. The dragon handled emotional support snacks.

It ended in tears, time magic, and applause.
As it should.

ACT IV: Realm X – The Realm of Rewrites:
The Curtain Rises (Against Everyone's Will)

Aurelya didn't remember signing up for a musical.

And yet here she was, centre stage, standing in a spotlight made entirely of sentient glitter, face-to-face with a squirrel in a cape who was holding a sword and judging her harshly.

Behind him, a raccoon orchestra warmed up with suspicious enthusiasm. A chorus line of possums stretched. The audience, a mix of goblins, bored fae, and one over-caffeinated goose, waited.

And then came the voice:

"YES, YES, LIGHT HER FROM BELOW! Give her that 'I've made horrible life choices' glow!"

Loki swirled onto the stage in a black velvet robe covered in sequins and despair. A director's headset clung to one horn, and he was inexplicably holding a clipboard, a megaphone, and a half-eaten éclair.

"Places, everyone! Act Two begins in fourteen seconds and we're doing it backwards, in interpretive dance, and possibly underwater! No time to explain, Aurelya, darling, you're the understudy for Emotional Closure. Dance like your trauma depends on it!"

Aurelya blinked.
She looked at Loki.
She looked at the squirrel.

And then she whispered to the dragon beside

her, "We're never getting out of this realm, are we?"

The dragon sighed. "Not unless you can out-sing a raccoon in a top hat."

INTERLUDE

PART II

TALES BETWEEN REALMS

THE QUIET BETWEEN THE LAUGHTER

Part II

Tales Between Realms

The Quiet Between the Laughter

Table of Contents – Part II

The Threads Between

A mysterious weaver collects whispers from across time.

In the stillness between realms, where time frays at the edges and yesterday sometimes forgets to end, their lives a weaver.

No one knows her name. Some say she is older than the realms themselves. Others say she is just very, very tired.

She sits beneath a sky stitched with too many stars, fingers moving faster than memory, threading golden strands of story through a loom made of bone and lullabies.

Each thread she touches hums, not with music, but with whispers: secrets, regrets, small kindnesses no one else noticed. She weaves them into a tapestry not meant to be seen but to be *felt* , the kind of magic that makes you pause at a familiar path you've never walked or dream of someone you've never met.

Sometimes, she laughs. Sometimes, she cries. Sometimes, she carefully removes a thread and replaces it with one that glows with a second chance.

The weaver does not speak. But if you sit with her long enough, in the hush of forgotten places, she might let you hold a single thread.

And if you’re very, very lucky, it might be yours.

Kaelun's Watch

A night in the life of a guardian who never sleeps.

The stars shift, and Kaelun watches.

He doesn't blink. Doesn't breathe. Doesn't *need* to.

The tower he guards overlooks all ten realms, though most cannot see it, not unless they're meant to. Tonight, the clouds whisper, and the moon hides behind them like a nervous child. It is not an ordinary night.

Kaelun adjusts the single stone at his side. It pulses softly, a rhythm only he hears. Below, the fabric of one realm trembles, a ripple of chaos, a tug of fate. He closes his eyes and listens to the echoes.

He remembers when the realms were one.

His armour hums with old runes and older memories. Every part of him is woven with oaths. He remembers *every* one.

A raven lands on the railing beside him. It says nothing. Neither does he. But they understand each other.

A child cries in the distance. A god stumbles through a choice. A dream forgets how to end.

And Kaelun watches.

Because if he doesn't, who will?

The God of Small Sorrows

A forgotten deity comforts the broken and unseen.

He is not worshiped.

There are no temples. No chants. No festivals in his name.

But he is always there, in the silence after someone is left behind. In the pause between sobs. In the sigh when the world forgets you.

The God of Small Sorrows does not roar. He does not smite. He does not demand.

He listens.

To the child who cries over a broken toy.
To the elder who sits alone as the seasons change.

To the dreamer who fears they will never be enough.
He mends what he can. With thread and time and gentle, invisible hands.

Sometimes he leaves a feather.
Sometimes a song only you can hear.
Sometimes just warmth, not from a fire, but from knowing someone saw you.

He is the god of forgotten things.
And he has not forgotten you.

The Trial of Loki

A ridiculous courtroom drama starring Loki as himself, and also as the prosecution.

Judge: "Will the real Loki please stand up?"

Three Loki's stood up.

One wore a monocle. One had a boa constrictor as a scarf. One was eating a croissant and looked mildly annoyed.

The jury, composed of a talking tree, a ghost horse, and a sentient puddle, stared in mild existential dread.

The prosecution (also Loki) dramatically adjusted his robes. "Ladies, gentlemen, and others, today we put Loki on trial not just for his crimes... but for his vibes."

Defence Loki (also Loki) scoffed. "Objection! That's incredibly vague."

Judge: "Sustained. But continue, I'm mildly entertained."

The evidence included:

- A flaming duck.
- A musical number.
- A squirrel witness who refused to speak without a glitter mic.

The trial lasted three days. On day two, someone summoned Odin as a surprise witness. Odin refused to testify without his coffee.

On day three, Loki cross-examined himself. The court transcripts read: "Snark, mischief, excessive self-awareness."

In the end, the jury ruled in favour of 'whoever brought the snacks.' Loki won.

Loki always wins. Even when he's losing.

Court adjourned to applause and one dramatic fainting goat.

No one remembers what the original charges were.

The Girl Who Said No to the Moon

They came to her window on the third night of her seventh year.

Whispers on the wind, silver-laced and full of promise. The kind of voice that smelled like moonflowers and sounded like the dream you forgot upon waking.

"Come with us," the moon said.

"No," said the girl.

It wasn't defiance. It wasn't fear. It was simply a truth she knew in her bones: she was not meant to follow.

The moon blinked or at least seemed to. No one had ever said no before.

The stars giggled nervously. A comet reversed direction just to make sure it heard correctly.

"No?" asked the night.

"No," the girl repeated, swinging her legs from the windowsill.

The moon tried again. "But we will show you galaxies. Teach you to name the dark. Wrap you in light and crown you with stories."

"I don't want to be a story," she said. "I want to live."

And that broke something.

In the distance, a prophecy fell off a shelf. Somewhere, a seer fainted. The river of fate paused its flow.

The girl turned away from the window and went back to bed. Her stuffed bear welcomed her with silent understanding.

The stars did not forget her.

Years later, they watched her grow into a woman who walked boldly, who defied oracles, who rewrote destinies.

But some nights , when the sky is especially still , the moon still waits outside her window.

Just in case she changes her mind.

The Cradle and the Sea

A sailor discovers a starlit realm hidden beneath the waves.

The sea was never quiet. It hummed with memory, whispered with longing, and called to those who knew how to listen.

She was one of them. A sailor by trade, but something else by blood. Her grandmother had told her stories as a child, tales of realms that shimmered beneath the tides, of stars that drowned to become pearls, and of gates that opened only under moonlight.

So when the storm came, she didn't steer away.

She followed it.

Lightning cracked. Waves rose like ancient gods. The crew screamed, but she smiled.

At the eye of the storm, where time stilled and water glittered with starlight, she found it: a spiral of light descending beneath the waves.

No air. No ship. Just her.

And the realm that had always whispered her name.

When she returned, days or decades later , no one was quite sure , she carried salt in her hair, a map in her skin, and a pearl that pulsed with the tide.

She never spoke of what she saw.

But on quiet nights, she would sing lullabies in a language older than time.

And the sea would answer.

The Ash and the Antlers

A memory from Kaelun's past, before Aurelya.

The forest was quiet in the way that only ancient places can be, where even the wind treads lightly, and time forgets itself.

Kaelun stood at the edge of a clearing, his antlers catching the last of the starlight. Before Aurelya. Before prophecy. Before everything that fractured him into more than just a sentinel.

He remembered the song.

It came on fog-bound nights like this, drifting through the trees on notes no mortal could replicate. It was the sound of memory without sorrow, hope without future. And it always led him here.

To her.

She wore silence like a cloak, bark braiding through her hair, and moss beneath her feet. Her eyes were galaxies buried in soil.

"You're late," she said, with the fondness of centuries.
"I was guarding the edges again," Kaelun replied.

"And who guards your edges?"

He never had an answer. Not then. Not ever.

The stag beside him, not a mount, but a companion, lowered its head in greeting to the woman who once made the stars pause. She ran a hand across its brow, then looked up at Kaelun with something that might have been sorrow… or might have been a warning.

"The threads are thinning," she said.

Kaelun nodded. "I know."

"Then why are you here?"

His reply came without thought. "Because I needed to remember who I was before I broke."

And for a moment, just one, he did.

He stepped forward.

The clearing accepted him.
The starlight held its breath.

A Flame Without a Name

A child born in the Realm of Flame remembers.

The flames did not burn her.

They whispered.

From the moment she opened her eyes, the fire spoke in crackles and hisses, telling stories no one else could hear. The other children cried when the sparks came close. She reached out and giggled as they danced across her fingers.

She was unnamed, unclaimed, a foundling left at the edge of the Ember Wells. The monks of the Flamewatch took her in, muttering about prophecy and trouble, but fed her all the same.

They called her Emberling.

By seven, she could walk across coals without a wince. By Ten, the torches bowed toward her when she entered the room. By twelve, the

High Flamekeeper warned the council: "The fire is listening to her. And worse, it seems to like her."

But the girl had no desire for power. Only for stories.

She spent her nights in the archives, coaxing half-burned scrolls back to life with careful heat and breath. The fire never consumed when she asked nicely.

And then, one night, it answered her.

In the deepest chamber, where the oldest flame burned, the First Spark, she whispered, "Who am I?"

The fire flared. And from it stepped a vision of a woman crowned in smoke and embers.

“My child,” the figure said, “you were not left behind. You were sent ahead.”

The flames pulsed with memory. And the girl , no longer just Emberling, knew she had a name. One the fire would keep safe until it was time.

A flame without a name. For now.

The Goat Who Would Be King

A tale of Thor's chicken-goat hybrid, destiny, and a very unqualified squirrel advisor.

Once upon a time , because that's the only way these things ever start , there lived a goat.

Except, it wasn't just a goat.

It had feathers.

And talons.

And an attitude that could only be described as "mildly possessed by chaos."

Thor, in one of his less lucid moments (which was saying something), had decided to improve on nature by combining his favourite animals: a goat and a chicken. The result was "Cluckles," a creature that defied taxonomy, decency, and basic laws of aviation.

Cluckles had dreams.

He also had a squirrel named Jibbers as his royal advisor.
Jibbers had no qualifications for this job, unless you counted the ability to yell "Viva la revolution!" while launching himself from chandeliers.

Thor, of course, thought this was all perfectly reasonable.

"It's about legacy!" Thor bellowed, draping Cluckles in a tiny cape stitched with runes of questionable translation. "The realms need a new leader! A new hope! A slightly confused barnyard dictator with feathers!"

Loki stared at the scene.

Then at Cluckles.

Then at Jibbers, who was now gnawing through a map of the nine realms.

"I'm not even surprised," Loki muttered. "I'm just… tired."

But the chaos couldn't be stopped.

Cluckles took to the campaign trail, which was less a trail and more a series of loud declarations made from rooftops.
Jibbers handled PR.

Posters appeared.

"Vote Cluckles: Because He Said So!"

"Feathers. Fury. Freedom."

"Peck the System."

The other realms watched in stunned silence.

And then , somehow , it worked.

Cluckles became King of Realm Three and instituted new laws, including mandatory midday naps, all-you-can-eat bug buffets, and formal tiaras for all goats.

Jibbers became Minister of Mischief and was last seen negotiating trade deals using acorns and interpretive dance.

Thor wept tears of pride.

Odin wept tears of confusion.

And Loki, ever the realist, just opened a betting pool on how long the monarchy would last. The answer: longer than expected.

And so, dear reader, if you ever hear distant squawking followed by the declaration of "All Hail King Cluckles!" , just bow.

It's safer that way.

Whispers in the Glass

A mirror learns what it means to reflect.

The mirror had seen centuries.

It had reflected queens at their cruellest, lovers at their most fragile, and children who didn't yet know what they feared. But never once, in all that time, had anyone asked the mirror how it felt.

Until her.

Aurelya didn't speak as she entered the chamber of glass. She didn't need to. Her eyes were full of a thousand unspoken stories. The mirror waited, humming with old enchantments, its surface shimmering faintly in her presence.
"You've seen everything," she finally

whispered.

The mirror pulsed.

"Yes," it replied, though its voice came not with sound, but with memory. It showed her a flash of laughter, a scream, a soft lullaby in a foreign tongue.
"I need to know what's true," she said.

The mirror didn't lie. But it didn't soften either.

And as Aurelya looked into it, into herself, it showed her every mask she had worn, every moment she had flinched, every truth she had swallowed to protect someone else.

She did not cry.

But she did nod.
"Thank you," she said.

And for the first time in centuries… the mirror felt seen.

The Garden Fracture

A story from the realm Aurelya never visited, and why.

There are realms that demand attention, all storm and shadow, glory and gold.
And then there are realms like the Garden.

The Garden didn't roar for recognition.
It didn't hunger to be remembered.
It simply… grew.

Once, long ago, Aurelya stood at its edge. One foot in, one foot out.
But something stopped her.
Not fear.
Not doubt.
Something older.

A whisper not from the trees, but from her

own bones:

"Not yet."

No maps marked it.

No names held it.

And yet, the Garden waited , not with longing, but with certainty.

Those who enter the Garden do not return unchanged.

And those who avoid it?

They carry questions that bloom in silence.

This is not Aurelya's story.

Not yet.

But the Garden remembers.

And one day, it will call again.

The Masked and the Missing

One of the Witnesses breaks their vow of silence.

In the forgotten folds of the tenth realm, where silence is law and memory itself treads lightly, one of the Witnesses stirred.

They had no name , only a mask etched with truths no one wanted to see.

They were never meant to speak.

But tonight, the stars flickered like nervous secrets, and the realm , stitched together by silence , trembled.

Aurelya arrived without warning. Her footsteps didn't echo, but the weight of her presence did. She bowed respectfully to the robed figure sitting in the temple's shadow.

"I'm not here to ask," she said. "I'm here to remember."

The Witness didn't nod. Didn't speak. But their hand moved, slowly, to remove the mask.

Underneath, there was no face. Just light. Flickering. Fractured. Familiar.

And then, like the unravelling of a forgotten thread, the Witness began to speak.

They told of the first fracture in the realms.

Of a love so bright it could only exist in shadow.

Of a child who should never have lived , and yet burned brighter than fate allowed.

Of names erased from scrolls, and of one name

whispered in defiance.

"Aurelya."

When they finished, the temple shook. Their vow was broken. The realm would remember.

And the stars, those ever-watching witnesses, wept softly in gratitude.

Meanwhile, in the Realm of Therapy

The realms go to group counselling. Chad the Goblin Life Coach returns.

Location: A folding chair circle in a suspiciously cozy cave.

Chad the Goblin Life Coach adjusted his lopsided spectacles and clicked his pen. "Okay, everyone, remember the rules: no interrupting, no incinerating your fellow attendees, and if you're going to shapeshift mid-share, please announce it for the transcript."

Present today:

• Thor (confused why he's here, brought snacks anyway)

• Loki (already lying on the chaise lounge, uninvited)

• A Sobbing Mirror (from Realm of Reflection)

• Gerald (still in a hoodie, mumbling about the 'unfairness of it all')

• A tree that may or may not be sentient (but has excellent posture)

• Aurelya (trying to vanish into her chair)

Chad clapped. "Let's begin! Who wants to share their progress since last session?"

Thor raised a hand. "I didn't smash anything this week. Just… cracked. A mug. Emotionally."

Loki rolled his eyes. "I summoned a phoenix to light my inner fire. It set my curtains on fire instead but still counts."

The mirror wept quietly. Chad handed it a box of tissues.

Gerald mumbled, "I wrote a poem. It rhymed with betrayal. A lot."

The tree rustled. Which Chad took as agreement.

"Wonderful progress!" Chad beamed. "Now let's try group trust falls. Thor, you're up first."

The session ended with laughter, mild injuries, and a group agreement to try hot yoga next time, except the tree, who refused to bend.

Chad's closing words: "Healing is messy. So is group therapy. But at least no one summoned a kraken this week. That's growth."

A Note from the Realms

Collected Post-Performance Reflections from

Those You Survived,

Loki

Stop reading this. You're emotionally compromised. That means I did my job. Also, I demand a standing ovation and a catered exit.

Nutters McFluff

Theatre changed me. I still chew stage curtains in my sleep. If you find a peanut under your pillow, I've been there. You're welcome.

P.S. Tell Gerald I'm not giving back the emotional support tiara.

Aurelya

I came here for answers. I left with raccoons, interpretive dance trauma, and a dragon who insists he's not emotionally invested. So… thank you, I think?

Sir Crumbs

No comment. My lawyer (a goose with anger issues) advised silence. But if you find tap shoes with glitter stuck to the laces , that's my signature.

Respect the sparkle.

Clarence

I didn't mean to speed-date the sea witch. She ordered for me. It was soup. I have regrets. Still single. Still majestic.

Gerald

Thank you for coming to my live crying circle. We raise our emotional support juice boxes to you. I'm proud of us. We made it, but we made it.

You're seen. You're valid. You're not alone.

Chad the Goblin Life Coach

If you've read this far, you've clearly been through some things. You're welcome at any group therapy bonfire in Realm 6. First marshmallows free.

WHERE'S MY TROPHY?!?
REALMSVERSE
TROPHY
YOR
QUIIFOING
CHUDY

About the Author

Holly Symons has always had one foot in mischief and the other in magic. Known for blending heartfelt storytelling with laugh-out-loud chaos, she built the Flameborn Presents series as a stage where sarcasm, sabotage, and the occasional sword-wielding possum can take a bow.

When she's not writing realms into existence (and accidentally breaking them in the process), Holly is usually surrounded by books, cups of tea she forgot to finish, and characters who refuse to stay in their own chapters. Her work is celebrated for its wit, theatrical flair, and unapologetically quirky heart a reminder that fantasy doesn't always have to be serious to be epic.

With Sarcasm, Sabotage & Other Misfires (Collector's Edition), Holly invites readers not just behind the curtain, but onto the stage itself chickens, glitter spills, and all.

REALMSVERSE
TROPHY
Outstanding Chaos

www.ingramcontent.com/pod-product-compliance
Lightning Source LLC
Chambersburg PA
CBHW042035180726
48295CB00006B/104

9781923567498